BLUFFTON

MY SUMMERS WITH BUSTER

MATT PHELAN

CANDLEWICK PRESS

First paperback edition 2017

Library of Congress Catalog Card Number 2012947260
ISBN 978-0-7636-5079-7 (hardcover)
ISBN 978-0-7636-8706-9 (paperback)

17 18 19 20 21 22 TLF 10 9 8 7 6 5 4 3 2

Printed in Dongguan, Guangdong, China

This book was typeset in Humana Sans.
The illustrations were done in watercolor.

Candlewick Press
99 Dover Street
Somerville, Massachusetts 02144

visit us at www.candlewick.com

For Nora and Jasper

Life in Muskegon, Michigan, was quiet. Ordinary.

1

But that all changed in the summer of 1908.

The summer *they* arrived.

The vaudevillians. Show people. Here to
spend the summer by our lake.

Bluffton was the name of the small neighborhood on the western bank of Muskegon Lake.

Bluffton was right by the last trolley stop at the foot of Pigeon Hill (the bluff). Everybody took that trolley because it was also the stop for Lake Michigan Park, a short stroll away.

Bluffton

Muskegon Lake

X

Lake Michigan Park

streetcar to Downtown Muskegon

Lake Michigan

My neighborhood

Of course, I'd been to Lake Michigan Park many times.

But I'd never been to Bluffton.

COBWEBS &
RAFTERS

OFFICIAL CLUBHOUSE
OF THE
ACTORS' COLONY

Sand breaks the fall.
It's like landing on a pillow.

27

28

29

Have a seat, young local yokel, and allow me, Ed Gray, Noted Monologuist, to elucidate on the subject at hand.

Here at the Actors' Colony, we have only the top talent, mind you. No medicine-show hucksters, road-show hacks, or tent-show miscreants here.

No, my good fellow, here we are the cream of the crop, the mainstays of the glorious two-a-day theaters, the pride of the Keith Circuit!

But I'm getting ahead of myself.

You say you've never seen a vaudeville bill?

Well . . .

Close your eyes and I shall paint you a mental picture.

Buster crawled onstage during his dad's act when he was but a babe. And he got a laugh. By age four, he was part of the act.

Whew! And WHAT an act!

The Three Keatons are the wildest knockabout act in the business.

They call Buster "the human mop."

The kid's indestructible. He can take a fall better than anyone alive.

And the kicker?

Buster never cracks a smile. Ever. No matter what. That's what really makes it funny.

And that is but a small taste of the glories of vaudeville.

Like I said, some of the biggest stars of all are here this summer enjoying the tranquility of Muskegon Lake, as the vaudeville houses are closed due to sweltering heat.

Last time the Three Keatons played Muskegon, Joe discovered Bluffton.

"Ed," he said to me, "it's a slice of heaven!"

Ain't it the truth?

44

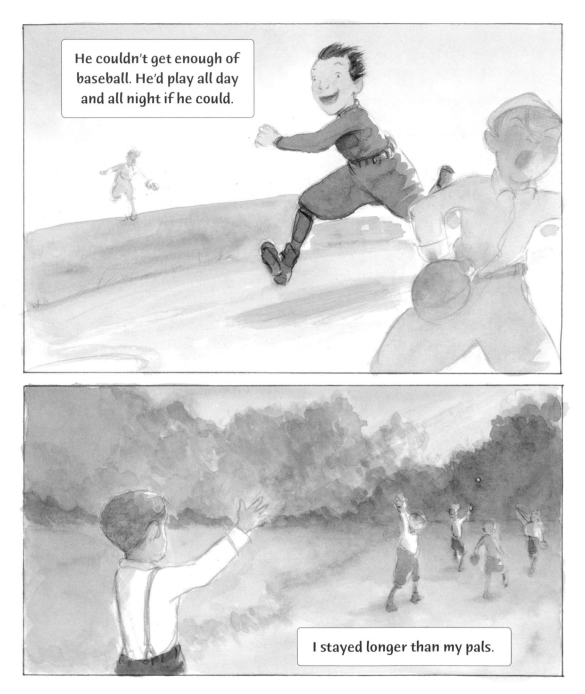

He couldn't get enough of baseball. He'd play all day and all night if he could.

I stayed longer than my pals.

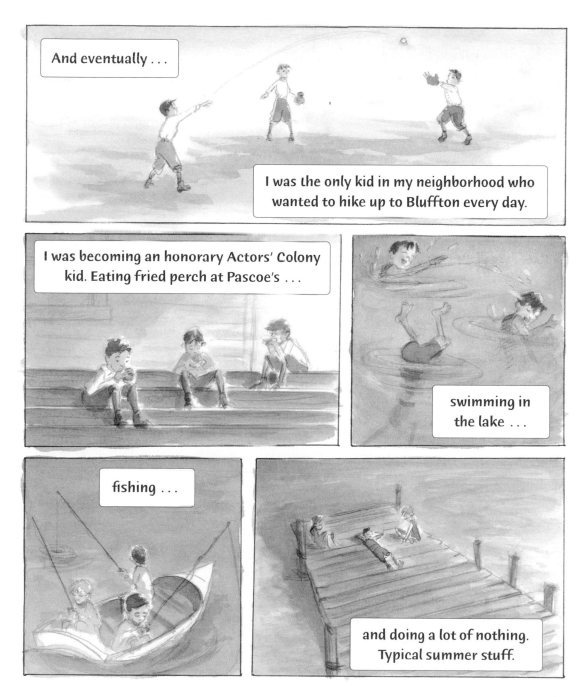

And eventually . . .

I was the only kid in my neighborhood who wanted to hike up to Bluffton every day.

I was becoming an honorary Actors' Colony kid. Eating fried perch at Pascoe's . . .

swimming in the lake . . .

fishing . . .

and doing a lot of nothing. Typical summer stuff.

But these weren't typical kids.

What about you, Lex?

Nah. I'm not in my folks' act. I just travel with 'em. Someday I'll be up there. Might be a monologuist or a comic. But I'll leave the falls to this knucklehead.

I'd be an acrobat if I could. But, you know, I'd have to learn some tricks.

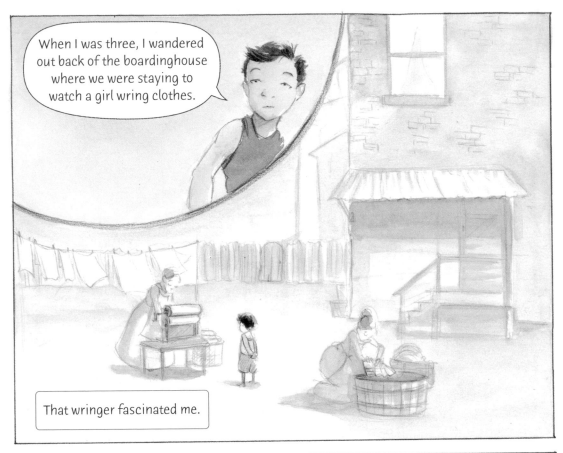

When I was three, I wandered out back of the boardinghouse where we were staying to watch a girl wring clothes.

That wringer fascinated me.

So I stuck my finger in it.

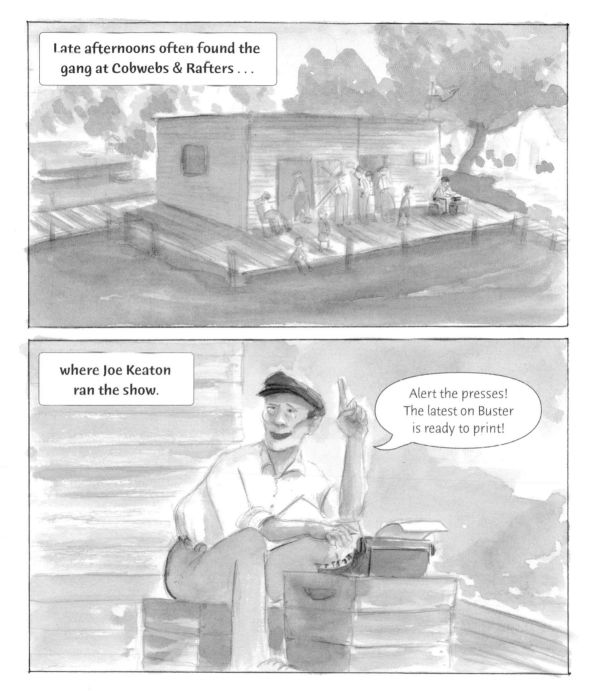

Late afternoons often found the gang at Cobwebs & Rafters . . .

where Joe Keaton ran the show.

Alert the presses! The latest on Buster is ready to print!

That summer held one more event of note.

Joe Keaton's birthday . . .

celebrated vaudeville style.

That was the first summer.

Occasionally, I'd get a letter from Lex, who was out on the road.

Buster never wrote.

Lex was traveling with his parents, so he got to watch all of the shows. He sent me detailed descriptions.

Lex often sent news of the Three Keatons, too.

They seemed to be having some trouble with the Gerry Society, an organization dedicated to protecting children from abuse.

Even when he was little, Buster had been dressed up to fool the authorities. Joe spread the rumor that he was a midget.

But lately, the Gerry Society had doubled their efforts.

And it fell to Joe Keaton to prove that Buster wasn't getting hurt in the act.

Lex told me in a letter that the Gerry Society had been successful.

Back in 1907, the Three Keatons had been banned from performing on the biggest New York stages for two years.

Buster hadn't mentioned that last summer.

Of course, Buster hadn't really talked about his life onstage at all.

Gee.

SUMMER, 1909

Bluffton picked up right where we left off the year before.

and added to the stories and mayhem at Cobwebs & Rafters.

The only difference was that there were even more vaudevillians this summer. They packed into the Bluffton Boardinghouse on Wilcox Street . . .

Buster's mom had plenty of friends for her constant pinochle game.

The days were again filled with baseball . . .

fishing for perch . . .

and loitering.

Buster hardly ever stopped. It was like he was trying to smush a whole summer into every single day.

Hi, Henry.

Hi, Sally. Hi, Mary. What are you doing?

101

The Keatons had started calling their cabin Jingles' Jungle because of Buster's brother's toys being everywhere. The cabin was sparse, no indoor plumbing or anything, but Buster loved it.

Jingles' Jungle is all we need.

Beats all the boardinghouses, that's for sure.

No summer would be complete without days spent at Lake Michigan Park, a short walk from the Bluffton trolley stop.

Everyone in Muskegon came to the park.

Sometimes the vaudevillians just couldn't help themselves.

Bill "Bojangles"
Robinson

And he's been hounded ever since. By the Gerry Society.

Now, Joe . . .

Protection of children. HA! Do you know how many poor kids are living on the streets of New York? Hungry every night? Orphans, kids kicked around by fathers who mean to hurt them. Do they save them? No! They bother us.

As the days went by, I'd try desperately to get Buster to show me more stunts and gags.

But he always changed the subject.

Most of the vaudevillians spent time practicing their acts.

145

Hello.

Oh! Hi, Henry. Buster's here.

I can see that.

Lemonade!

I hope you like oatmeal cookies, Buster dear.

Henry.

I didn't know exactly why I said what I said.

I was mad.
Mad at Buster.
Mad at myself.

Mad about everything he had . . .

Everything I wanted.

before I returned.

Lex told me that Buster had been spending a lot of time playing with his little brother lately.

And playing ball with the grown-ups.

Something else had happened while I was away. . . .

Summer went on. Everyone said that Bluffton wasn't the same without the Keatons.

Cobwebs & Rafters seemed sparser and far less lively.

The letters from Lex stopped arriving.

Sometimes I would go to the library and read the vaudeville newspapers.

I learned that the Keatons' tour of England had been cut short. Apparently, Joe didn't like the food.

At any rate, their New York ban was lifted and they were back starring in the biggest venues.

BUSTER IS SIXTEEN!

NEW YORK—Vaudeville sensation "Buster" Keaton has reached the grand old age of sixteen. A performer since he was knee-high to a ventriloquist, "Buster" has performed in the finest venues of the vaudeville circuit. As the star of The Three Keatons, "Buster" has been often respectfully referred to as The Human Mop.

That's not true. He just turned fourteen. His father lies about his age to fool the authorities.

I know.

Well . . . see you, Henry.

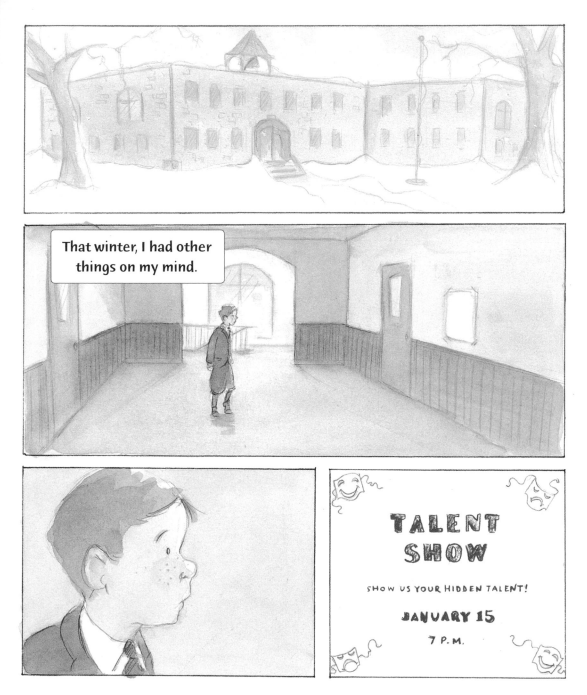

That winter, I had other things on my mind.

TALENT SHOW

SHOW US YOUR HIDDEN TALENT!

JANUARY 15

7 P.M.

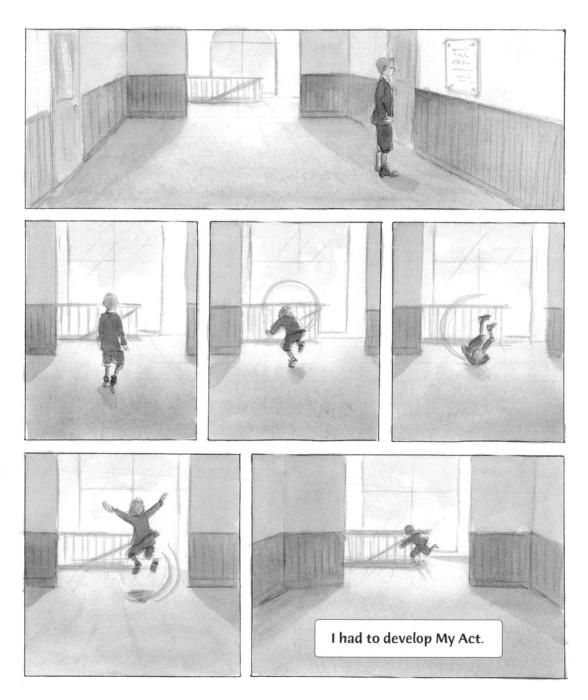

I had to develop My Act.

170

177

THUD!

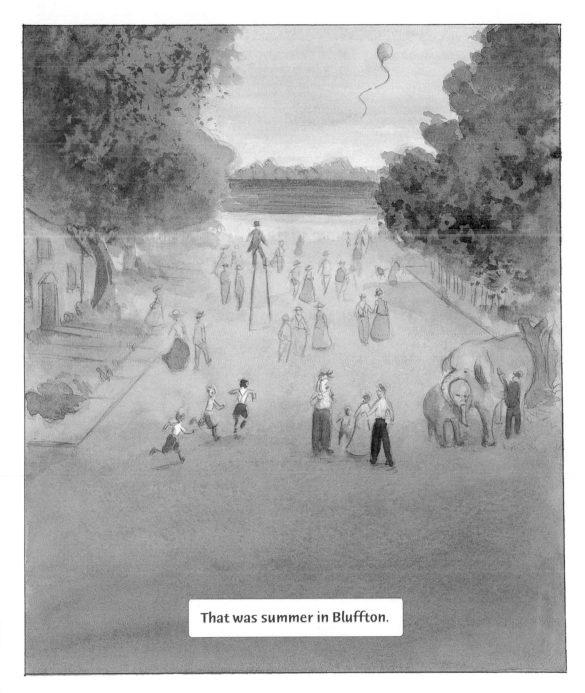

That was summer in Bluffton.

I bought a small theater near Bluffton and turned it into a movie house.

Now I provide entertainment for everyone in town.

I play all kinds of movies, but folks prefer the comedies.

For a couple of hours, they can relax, laugh, and forget about their day-to-day lives.

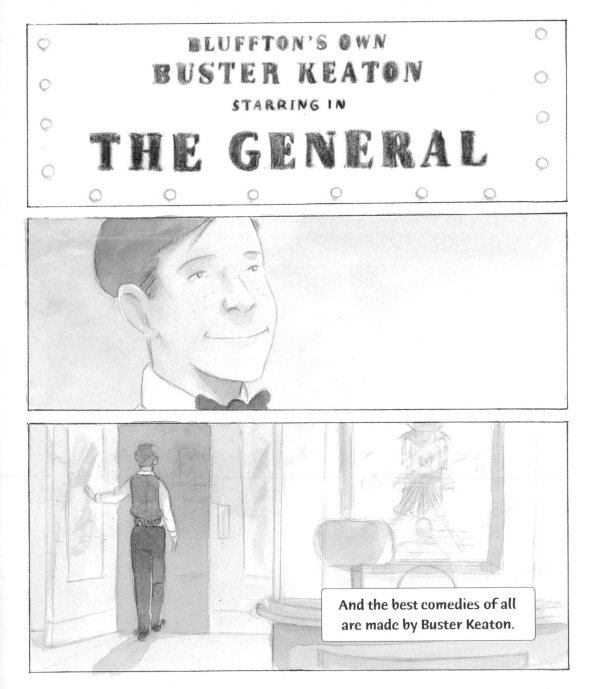

BLUFFTON'S OWN
BUSTER KEATON
STARRING IN
THE GENERAL

And the best comedies of all are made by Buster Keaton.

AUTHOR'S NOTE

Although Henry, Sally, and their families are fictional characters, Buster Keaton and the rest of the vaudevillians were real people. The Actors' Colony at Bluffton, which Joe Keaton founded, existed in Muskegon, Michigan, from 1908–1938. For many years the Keatons were central figures in Bluffton. Buster decided to end the family act in his late teens. He was about to embark on a solo career in vaudeville when he was invited by his friend Roscoe Arbuckle to give the (still relatively new) movies a try. Buster never looked back. He moved to Hollywood and brought his family with him. While this was the beginning of a great era for him professionally, it brought an end to the Keatons' summers in Muskegon.

Buster never forgot Bluffton or his old friends. Lex Neal joined Buster in Hollywood and worked as a writer on some of his movies. Big Joe Roberts and Joe Keaton acted in many of his short films. Buster's movies feature elaborate contraptions and gags, some of which can be traced back to the pranks he concocted during his boyhood summers. While making his movies, Buster would often stop the cameras so that everyone could play a quick game of baseball.

All of Buster's movies are readily available for viewing, and I highly recommend them. They are hilarious, breathtaking, innovative, and will change the way you think about silent films. Buster was a true genius, and his work stands the test of time. In 2007, the American Film Institute included Keaton's *The General* in its list of the 100 greatest American films ever made (it ranked at number 18).

I have been a fan of Buster Keaton since I was a small boy. My brother and I would watch *Cops* and *The General* projected on a bedroom wall by my dad's Super 8 film projector. At first, I just thought he was funny. Then I marveled at the amazing stunts he executed. And then, eventually, I realized he was simply one of the greatest actors and filmmakers who had ever lived. I read everything I could about Buster, including his autobiography, *My Wonderful World of Slapstick*. That is where I discovered the inspiration for this book.

For all his many accomplishments, Buster would always say that the happiest days of his life were those summers he spent at Bluffton.

A teenage Buster in front of Cobwebs & Rafters. Second from the left is
Joe Keaton. Big Joe Roberts is behind Buster and Ed Gray is on the far right.

(Date and photographer unknown. From the collection of the author.)

a graphic novel by
Matt Phelan

The Dust Bowl is
sweeping through 1937
Kansas and eleven-
year-old Jack Clark
isn't sure he can trust
what he sees — or that
he can be a hero.

MATT PHELAN
THE STORM IN THE BARN

★ "A masterpiece." — *Booklist* (starred review)

★ "Simply stunning." — *The Horn Book* (starred review)

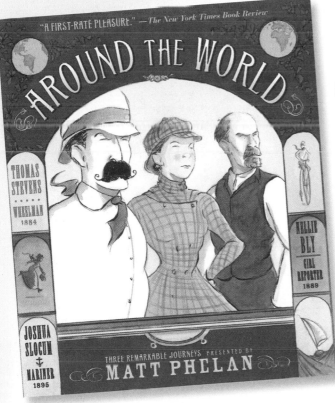

a graphic novel by
Matt Phelan

As the nineteenth century wound down, a public inspired by Jules Verne's novel *Around the World in Eighty Days* clamored for intrepid adventure. These three hardy spirits rose to the challenge.

"A first-rate pleasure." — *The New York Times Book Review*

★ "Three true tales of adventure as grand and admirable in the telling as they were in the doing." — *Kirkus Reviews* (starred review)

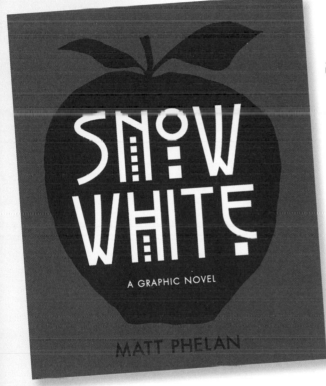

MATT PHELAN is the author-illustrator of several critically acclaimed graphic novels, including the Scott O'Dell Award–winning *The Storm in the Barn*; *Around the World*, which was nominated for two Eisner awards; and *Snow White*. He is the author-illustrator of the picture book *Druthers* and the illustrator of many books for young readers, including *Marilyn's Monster* by Michelle Knudsen; *Always* and *I'll Be There*, both by Ann Stott; *Miss Emily* by Burleigh Mutén; and *The Higher Power of Lucky* by Susan Patron, winner of the Newbery Medal. Matt Phelan lives in Pennsylvania.